HuGLeSS DouGLAS AND THE BIG SLEEP

DaVID MeLLING

A division of Hachette Children's Books

Hodder Children's Books

Rabbit's House

Douglas was packing all his things for Rabbit's sleepover. He had a lot of stuff but there was plenty of room at Rabbit's. He packed his honeybee pyjamas, a toothbrush and a storybook.

He was very excited!

'I hope Rabbit reads a bedtime story,' thought Douglas as he set off into the woods. His bag was very heavy with all his things. First he got stuck and then he got lost.

He climbed up the nearest tree to see where he was.
Only the tree he chose was quite thin and...

...bendy!

Douglas crashed to the ground and nearly squashed Little Sheep!

'Hello,' said Douglas. 'I'm going to Rabbit's for a sleepover, but I'm lost.'

'I know the way,' Little Sheep squeaked.

Douglas smiled. 'Why don't you come along too? **THERE'S PLENTY OF ROOM AT RABBIT'S.'**

Douglas scrambled out of the bush and brushed himself down.

'Funny,' he thought, 'my bag feels even heavier now.'

At last they arrived at Rabbit's house.
'Twoooooo twit! You won't fit!' Owl hooted.

'I only brought one little friend,'
said Douglas, 'and there's plenty
of room at Rabbit's.'

Rabbit's House

'What about us?' cried the sheep.

Rabbit was very happy to see everyone.
'I love having sheep over for sleepovers,' she laughed,
and she waved them all into her house,
one by one by one.

'Your front door does look small,' baaed Little Sheep.
'Nonsense!' said Rabbit. 'There's plenty of room.'

Poor Douglas.

They pushed…

…and they pulled.

'I don't think this is working,' Douglas said.
'Wait a minute!' cried Rabbit, snapping her fingers.
'I'll dig a bigger hole.'

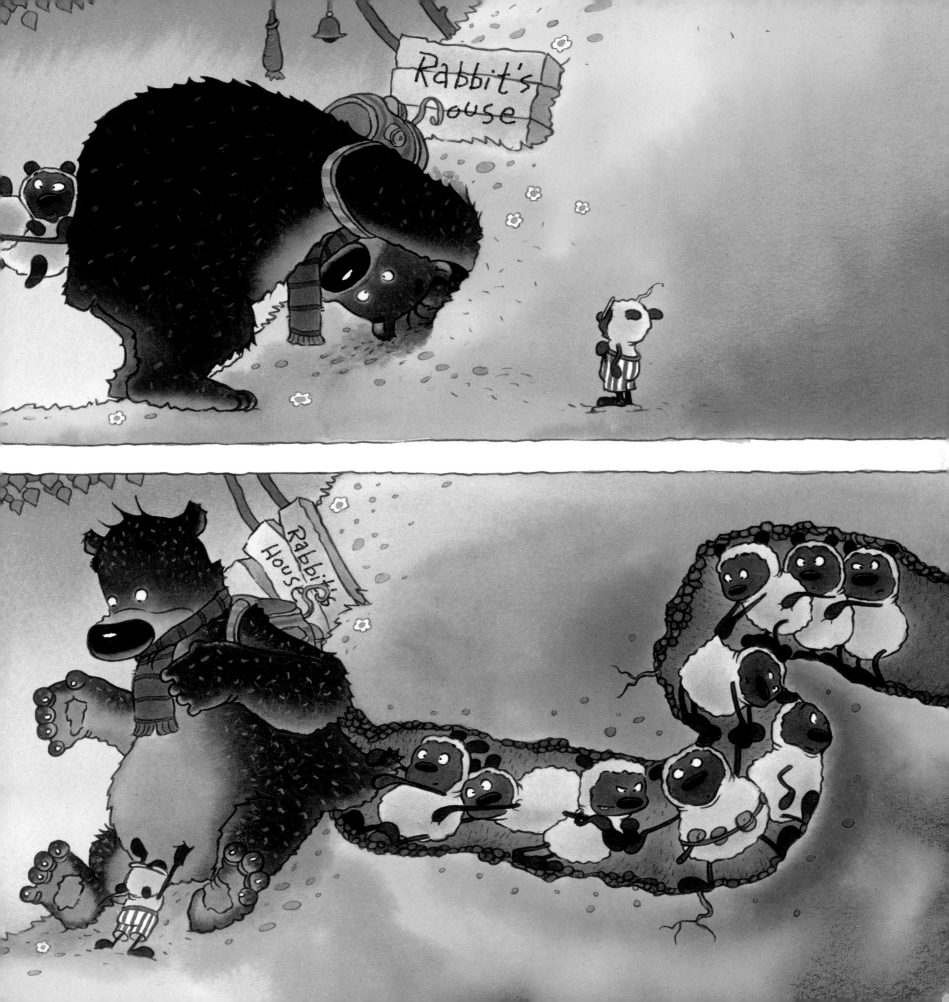

'There now,' puffed Rabbit. 'Isn't that cosy?'
Douglas wasn't so sure.

'When are you going to read us a bedtime story, Rabbit?' asked Little Sheep.

'As soon as I get in,' Rabbit replied. 'Budge up!'

Everyone shuffled and nudged and squeeeeeeezed about.

'THERE'S NO MORE ROOM AT RABBIT'S!' cried Douglas.

Little Sheep brushed his tickly fleece against Douglas' big round nose.

'AA-AA-AT...

Out popped the sheep, one... two... three...

four... five... six... seven... eight... nine... ten!

There were sheep all over the place.

Douglas gathered them together
and looked around.

'There's plenty of room out here,' he said.

zzzzzzzzzzz

So Douglas and the sheep settled down and listened
to Rabbit read a story.
'Once upon a time,' Rabbit began, 'there was a big, big
sleepover...'
And, one by one, they all closed their eyes and fell asleep.

What would you pack for a sleepover?

Slippers

Glow-in-the-dark gadgets

Pyjamas

Blanket

Storybook

Toothbrush

Woolly socks

Teddy bear